DAREDEVILS

BY ANNE GREENE

Micah 6:8b-What doth the Lord require of thee, but to do justly, and to love mercy, and to walk humbly with thy God.

To Darlene,
Joy and Peace,
Anne Greene

Written by: Anne Greene

Published by: Forget Me Not Romances, a division of Winged Publications

ISBN-10:1-944203-90-7

ISBN-13:978-1-944203-90-0

CHAPTER 1

1925 – Kill Devil Hills, North Carolina

Gloria Richards didn't have time to cry anymore. She scrubbed her hands over her wet cheeks, fluffed her bobbed hair, and straightened her shoulders.

If only she had family, then she wouldn't feel so alone.

Her blonde rescue puppy tilted her head and gazed up with adoring brown eyes.

"You're sweet, Daisy, but I need more family than you."

Gloria plodded from the bathroom into the bedroom. "Daisy, we've no food in the cottage, so I need to have a heart-to-heart chat with Mr. Rand

Maitland. He's exactly the type of older man I prefer to work with." No more fending off amorous bosses. "I need to find another partner like Buzz." A tear slipped from her eye and wiggled down her cheek. "I miss you, Buzz. If you were still alive, I wouldn't be in this mess. Thanks to Vincent and his lies, no other pilot will hire me."

The small shaggy puppy bowed her front knees and wagged her tail so hard her entire body shook.

"Sorry. I can't play just now." Gloria swiped a fist across her cheek and snagged her only dress from a hanger, leaving the small closet empty. "I'll force myself to be amusing and cheerful. Older men like that." Anything to improve her chance of getting a job. According to Annie, Rand Maitland had been an ace fly boy during the war. She could trust his acrobatics.

Daisy's tail thumped on the linoleum bedroom floor.

Gloria turned on the radio. The latest hit burst through the static. *"Ev'ry morning, ev'ry evening, Ain't we got fun? Not much money, Oh! But honey! Ain't we got fun?"*

Belting out the words, Gloria perched on the edge of the sagging bed, pulled shiny, silk stockings just above her knees and rolled in the garters. If she sang long enough, the song might raise her droopy spirits.

She stood and slid into the white dress that ended in a shocking way just below her knees. Well, older men liked that too. She'd need every advantage to capture this job.

Suited her just fine she didn't need to flatten her bosom because God hadn't overly endowed her. In her line of work a voluptuous bust got in the way. She reached behind her back to zip up her dress. Easy, because the fabric draped open to below her shoulder blades in the rear. Scandalous in the daytime, but she only had this one gown or her trousers. "Trousers won't impress the old man, Daisy, and I can't wear my costume. Being broke is just tedious."

She smoothed the drop-waist dress and settled on the edge of the bed to slip on red, high-heeled shoes. She stood and pivoted in front of the blonde puppy. "How do I look?"

Daisy slid to her butter-ball stomach, hind legs splayed.

Gloria reached down to pet the silken head.

Daisy gave her a puppy smile.

Gloria blew out her breath. If only she had a bigger mirror than the small vanity above the bathroom sink. She shrugged and grabbed her gloves and hat. "You be a good girl and don't make a mess while I'm gone."

Daisy crouched on her haunches, head tilted and brown eyes sad.

"I know you don't like to be left alone. I'll be back before you can find the puppy treat I hid."

Though her might-be-new boss lived close, she'd borrow Annie's Model T roadster. "Rand Maitland's bound to have his Jenny tied-down near the sand runway, and I don't want to get grit inside my only pair of dress shoes."

Daisy raised a paw to be shaken.

Gloria smiled, bent and shook the furry offering.

She didn't need the auto since Kitty Hawk wasn't more than five hundred yards or so from Annie's cottage near Kill Devil Hills, but Mr. Maitland would be more impressed if she drove. He mustn't know how desperately she needed this job or he wouldn't hire her.

Her high heels tapped a determined rhythm on the uneven linoleum as she crossed the living room. She shut the door behind her and marched down the rickety wooden stairs to the beach. Stepping carefully to keep loose sand out of her shoes, she tiptoed around the cottage to where Annie had parked her Model T before she left for Europe.

Gloria bent, cupped the crank handle on the front of the car in her palm, pulled the choke wire with her left hand and gave the crank a quick half-turn. The engine sputtered to life. Her shoes slipped on the sandy driveway as she minced on tip-toes around to the driver's seat and climbed inside.

Thank You, Father, for this quick-start engine. Setting her jaw, she steered down the hard-packed sand that passed for a road toward Kitty Hawk.

She glanced in the rearview mirror, frowned and snapped her fingers. Already close to the three bi-planes tied down just beyond a cluster of larger cottages on stilts, it was too late to turn back. She'd forgotten to apply that new chalk-white face powder that was all the rage. Nor had she painted her lips red. She'd wanted that color to bolster her confidence and hide her pain. She shook her head and shrugged. Well, she had a stiff spine and didn't need to paint on courage.

She pulled up next to the closest home, stopped the automobile, turned off the ignition, set the brake, and slipped out the door. Just off the road, her red high-heeled shoes sank into loose sand. "Ain't we got fun?" she murmured dryly. Her shoes had survived worse obstacles. These red high heels would outlast this setback too.

In the slanting morning light, three visiting bi-planes cast long shadows. All the other planes, snug inside hangars, waited for tomorrow's barnstorming show.

A man wearing blue coveralls with his back to her, bent over the engine casing of the middle Jenny. Annie mentioned Mr. Maitland named his plane *Jazzman*, so that big fella had to be the man himself, right where she thought she'd find him.

Taking giant steps through the sifting sand between her and the hard-packed sand beneath the Jennies, she stopped directly behind him. She tugged her red cloche hat low over one eyebrow, held down the silky skirt flapping in the breeze, and straightened her shoulders.

"Hello!" She highlighted her voice to sound

perky. Older men liked perky.

The man grunted, tightened a bolt on the engine with a large wrench and then turned.

She started, her hands flew up, and she almost lost her footing. Annie hadn't mentioned her husband's youngest brother was gorgeous.

He flashed a smile.

Dimples played around that dazzling grin and found an immediate place in her heart. He stared at her with eyes bluer than the bluest lapis. And he was no older man.

Too bad for her. She pressed her lips together. She'd so counted on Mr. Maitland being older. She'd learned her lesson about handsome men, and she better make sure she remembered it.

****

Rand planted the wrench on the engine casing, held out his hand, and then immediately withdrew the greasy thing. He reached for the rag in his rear pocket and wiped both palms until the grease vanished. Then he extended his hand again. "Hello, I'm Matthew Randolph Maitland, Jr. And you are?"

She was stunning. But she had to be one of those frivolous flappers because she wore the wrong clothes for the breezy, sunny beach. Her shoes sank almost ankle deep in the blowing sand, and she had to clutch her knees to hold that shining dress down. When the hem fringes blew, the dress shimmered.

Beneath that crazy, red cap, blonde hair fluttered around the most agreeable face he'd ever laid eyes on. He swallowed. Those surprised big eyes, the color of a gray mist, could haunt his dreams. If he hadn't been holding her hand, warm and soft against his callouses, he'd think she was an apparition.

"I'm Gloria Richards. Good to meet you."

The throaty voice sent shivers down his spine. "What can I do for you?" He glanced at the shiny black automobile parked on the road. "Auto trouble?" His hand moved to the wrench.

She smiled.

His heart missed a couple beats.

"No. I came to talk with you."

"Yeah?" She belonged at a coming-out party in a fancy country club where she'd be surrounded by men sporting white tails and carnations in their buttonholes. He pulled in a deep breath. The pungent fumes of gasoline brought him down to earth, and made his aching head pound. He knew her kind. He'd met his belly full of spoiled debutantes. But this one had something winsome about her.

"I'm Annie Maitland's friend."

"Annie? Curt's wife?" Rand scratched his head. "Oh, yeah. You're the Richards girl. I've heard of you." What had he heard? Didn't pay much attention to girl talk. Something about her being an orphan, bobbing her hair, and wearing cosmetics ... though that clear skin didn't look made-up. But what did he know?

"Could we go somewhere to talk?" She waved a

graceful hand, then quickly swiped both palms down across her flying skirt.

“Sorry, but I’ve got a lot of work before the show tomorrow.” Did she think he could stop everything and take her across the inlet to the Blue Crab? “What’s on your mind?”

She was a bright thing and looked to have plenty of energy and pizzazz. But his words deflated the aura of radiance around her. He clenched his jaw. Blast his flat wallet. He wasn’t a cad. If she needed to talk, he’d take her somewhere cool and comfortable ... if he could.

She glanced up and down the beach, empty except for the sleeping houses that announced the outskirts of Kitty Hawk, and then nodded toward the Model T. “We could sit in the auto.”

Umm...that wasn’t going to happen. Not in a Tin Lizzie. Judging by the weakness in his knees he’d fall under her spell the minute he sat on the plush seat next to her. “I’m busy.” He half-turned away and caught the scent of something sweet hovering around her. “Just tell me what you want.” His voice had turned husky. He cleared his throat. “I’ve got work to do.”

She took a step closer and frowned. “Please, this is hard enough without you making it more difficult.”

Once again that throaty voice riveted him. With a voice like that she had to be a song bird. With her looks she’d pack ‘em in at Sam’s Speakeasy. He pushed a heavy hand though his hair. Hard for her?

What did she know? How many times did a man look up from a bad job and discover a beautiful woman standing behind him? He shoved his hands into his pockets. She had spirit. He admired a woman with backbone, even if she was one of those new-fangled flappers. "Okay, shoot."

A small frown wrinkled her forehead. "Since you've heard of me, you know I'm a wing walker."

His shoulders stiffened. Whoa! Impossible! This sprite of a girl! "I don't believe you," he spouted before he clamped his lips. He dug his hands out of his pockets, picked up the wrench, turned to the plane, and pretended to tighten a nut on his wing. This had to be a joke. He'd only been back in town one day and already the guys were setting him up. Another one of their practical jokes.

"You heard Buzz Greenwood took a nosedive?"

He nodded, keeping his eyes on the engine. Looking at her rattled his brains.

"He was my pilot. *Silver Lining* was our plane."

He jerked his head up.

She blinked those gray, misty eyes against sparkling tears.

He tightened his grip around the wrench to keep from patting her on the shoulder. He turned back to tighten his wing nut, swabbed off a few drops of excess grease and then swiveled back toward her. "The guys are carrying this prank too far." He'd rub their faces in their joke. "What are you, some kind of actress?" He winked.

"Actress?" She heaved an exasperated-sounding sigh.

Those misty, gray eyes had turned as hard as ice picks.

"No. I'm a wing walker. The best wing walker on the east coast. If you hadn't just blown in for the Nags Head Barnstorm, you'd have heard of me." A definite jaw line angled her soft face.

She wanted to walk his wing?

She yanked off her smart hat and raised the soft thing as if she intended to hit him with it. Blonde curls glowed in the sunlight. Her dress flapped higher. She swatted the fringe down.

She wanted to walk *his* wing!

Why was he sweating like a rookie pilot? Him! He mopped his forehead with the grease rag. So that was her angle. "Buzz and the *Silver Lining* crashed two days ago. They're memories. It's sad but accidents happen all the time. Barnstorming's a risky profession. We all take that chance."

Curt had mentioned that Buzz had a swanky wing-walker, but he'd not paid any attention, been too busy thinking of his last several months down at Wilmington finalizing his real estate deal. He swallowed. He'd been out of barnstorming far too long. Time to get sharp again.

Sweat beaded between his shoulder blades. "Okay, say I believe you. I don't need a wing walker. I'm a pilot. I do stunts. I'm a solo performer. I don't play second fiddle to anyone."

"Sure, you do aerial stunts during your show, but you need more air time." She tilted her small, triangular chin high. "I'll sit in the co-pilot's seat until your act's over, and then I'll crawl out onto your wing, and you can fly for my act."

"Unbelievable!" He turned away. "You want to butt in on my act and take over."

She put a hand on his arm. "Just listen for a minute."

Okay, he could give her that. He braced his back against the fuselage and crossed his arms.

She took a deep breath that puckered her lips. "I do it all, ballet on the wing, hang on a rope ladder by my teeth, switch from one plane to another in mid-air, and do handstands. There's not a trick invented that I don't perform." She batted thick eyelashes.

His stomach did funny loop-de-loops. He knew what she was doing, yet ...

"And, we can invent new ones." She smiled.

He propped an elbow on the wing. He had to scram before she had him drooling. He had no place in his life for another woman. None. One proved too many. He'd lost all respect for his older brother when Annie tamed Curt. And look how a wife grounded Judd. And any spirit Dad had, Mom suppressed years ago. He was the only pilot left of the famous Maitland Brothers. Rand shook his head. No female would demolish him that way. Not today. Not even after he set the world record. Not ever.

One female in his life already tangled him with too many complications.

He didn't need another debutant like the one Dad was bent on chaining him up with. Discouraging one woman was bad enough, he didn't need another ritzy dish messing up his life.

He threw the dirty rag onto the cantankerous engine. He'd worked his way to where he stood on the threshold of flying further, faster, and higher than Charlie Lindbergh and Wiley Post. Rand Maitland *would* set the world's record. Another woman in his life could slow him down. Or stop him.

Come hurricane or high water, he *would* set the world flight record. He'd fly around the world.

And for sure, women cost too much money. He barely had a dime to rub against a nickel that wasn't tied up in *The Jazzman* and real estate venture.

Plus, this flapper couldn't be as good as she painted herself.

The fellas had to be pulling a fast one. She was too good to be true. And when something was too good to be true—it wasn't. He jumped up on the wing and climbed into the pilot's seat. If there had been a door, he would have slammed it.

He called, "Hey, Blondie, spin the prop, will ya?"

He liked life just the way it was. He didn't need any more upsets. If he hired this sweetheart, she would turn his world upside down and topple his ambition.

Chapter 2

Oh, dear Father God, my whole life's fallen apart. Please help me.

Gloria laid her Bible on the slanting edge of the three-legged table, jumped up from the lumpy rattan sofa, and padded barefoot the few feet to the beach cottage's tiny bathroom. She splashed her face with cold water. Her blood-shot eyes and fiery nose reflected back to her from the vanity mirror. She grabbed a towel. The worn, white cloth scratched her face.

Daisy gazed up with mournful puppy-dog eyes.

"Well, I won't cry anymore." She blew her nose. "Not for Buzz and not for the Jenny bi-plane." She slapped her hands on her hips. "Do you know how that awful Rand Maitland phrased it?"

Daisy thumped her tail.

"He said Buzz and the Jenny are memories.

Have you ever known anyone so awful?"

Daisy rolled over on her back exposing her pink-skinned pot belly.

Gloria knelt and rubbed the warm tummy. "Buzz and that vintage war plane meant so much more than that to me." She nuzzled her face with Daisy's furry paw. Tears cascaded into the soft fur.

She tightened her lips. Driving Annie's Model T to the horrible crater in the sand dune where Buzz crashed had been a mistake. She couldn't erase the burn site from her mind. She stood and hung the towel on the ring beside the sink. "He must have flown too low so the onlookers could get a clear view of his spiral, and the Jenny stalled."

Daisy's toenails scrabbled on the black-specked linoleum as she rolled over and leaped to her feet.

Gloria tugged on her panties and Bandau Brassiere. Had she neglected to change *Silver Lining's* oil? Had she missed something vital while testing that old engine? Was Buzz's crash her fault?

"Not much money, but oh honey. Ain't we got fun!" she belted, her voice morning-frog-raspy. Today, singing the cheerful song didn't help. She pulled on over-size coveralls. Her bare feet slapped the linoleum floor as she ambled from the bathroom to the small living room.

When she stopped, Daisy's cool, wet nose touched her heels.

"No, I checked that engine the day before." She reached down to pet Daisy's soft, flappy ears. "That freaky kind of accident happens far too often to barnstormers." She crumpled her wet hanky, stuck the wad into the pocket of her coveralls, and shambled to the small front window.

"I didn't cause the accident, Daisy! I really, really didn't. But knowing that doesn't change anything. Buzz is still dead."

"Woof."

She would have been wing-walking on his Jenny if she hadn't performed a triple show the day before. Good-old Buzz gave her the day off. She sniffed and blinked against the tears that dripped, though she forbade them.

Gloria pressed her nose to the sand-speckled glass of the cottage's front window. Outside, pink streaks of sunrise sparkled troubled aqua-blue water. Wisps of fog rose over damp sand. The beach appeared as empty and foreboding as her life.

Her stomach rumbled.

No need to visit the ice box. The small battered unit contained only a glass bottle with less than one inch of milk and a quarter head of lettuce. If she ate breakfast the small unit would be empty except for the chunk of ice melting in its compartment.

She took the last Milk Bone from the box, dropped the tidbit into Daisy's bowl and set the treat out for her. "There you go, Daisy." After crumpling the box, she threw the carton into the trash can under the sink.

Crunch, crunch, crunch. The tiny sound filled

the miniature kitchen.

Gloria ran her fingers through her short hair and lifted the locks from her neck. Surprising how she missed the long, heavy tresses she'd shorn because they interfered with work. Oh well, cutting off her crowning glory was the least of her worries.

A sigh struggled up from deep inside her chest. Well, this day wouldn't wait around for her to grieve. Time to lift her chin and get on with life.

No need to peek into her pocketbook. The change purse was empty. Buzz hadn't had a chance to pay her.

His wife, Mattie, and the twins needed whatever money Buzz managed to sock away. Gloria swiped at her eyes. The ten-year old girls would really miss their daddy. Buzz lavished all his spare time on the twins. She had spent a lot of time with them too.

She wouldn't ask Mattie for her share. Dear old Buzz had been more Dad than boss. Tomorrow, she'd smother her tears and run over to their bungalow to see what she could do to help. Today, she had that nasty job to do.

"You love those girls, don't you, Daisy. I'll take you with me tomorrow. The twins enjoy playing with you."

Daisy whined at the door.

Gloria's shoulders heaved. Living without a daddy provided a one-way route on Mean Street. Her feet had travelled each familiar rut and pothole. At least the twins had their mom. If only she could remember her mother's face. Sometimes at night in a dream, she could almost see the wavering image. But always she woke before her mother's features grew clear.

Daisy gave a short bark.

Gloria blinked hard, opened the door and let Daisy out.

The puppy sniffed around in the sand at the base of her favorite scraggly bush.

Gloria leaned her forehead against the door jamb and forced herself to stop sniffling. She'd stick close to Abby and Aggie as long as the twins needed her. She couldn't love them more if they'd been her sisters.

Her stomach growled.

She set her jaw. Mourning for Buzz was over. Time to face that stinking job.

Annie's husband's youngest brother and a few other men still had their Jennies tied down at Kitty Hawk. She must try again with that dreadful Rand Maitland. No use attempting to find work with anyone else. Thanks to Vincent, behind her back every local pilot called her the nickname that made her unemployable. No locals would hire her.

She had to convince Maitland. She couldn't take no for an answer. He was her last option. *Oh, Lord, why couldn't he be old or at least nice?*

She must persuade that distasteful man or sing again at Sam's Speakeasy. Since Sam insisted on more than her performing on stage, working with that blotto woman-chaser wasn't even a choice.

And there was no other work for a woman in all of Kitty Hawk.

That left only Mr. Rand Maitland, ace pilot of the Great War.

****

Rand poured another cup of coffee and shuffled across the bright new black and white tile squares to settle at the new-fangled Formica table. Rays from the rising sun filtered inside the bungalow and played shadow and sunlight tag on the gray-swirled table-top.

He gulped the hot brew. Didn't help. He lowered his aching head into cupped hands and massaged his scalp. He'd tried the new Bayer Aspirin twice. The four white tablets had eased his headache, but still his temples pounded like an engine with a cracked piston. The third cup of coffee hadn't eased his pain either.

He was in no shape to fly today, but what was new? As long as no one discovered his blind eye he would fly. No headache would ground him. Maybe he'd skip the head pounding- loop-de-loop today. The acrobatics increased the pain exponentially. Yesterday, he'd been so dizzy after he landed he'd pretended to check out his instruments until the fuzziness eased and he could see straight. When he climbed out, he almost upchucked.

He would fly as long as the pain didn't cause blackouts or endanger his audience.

Usually the pain abated before he flew again. Maybe not today. Headaches seemed to be getting more frequent and lasting longer.

His disability pension from the Great War didn't amount to much. Not more than paying for a week's groceries. He rubbed a hand over his morning whiskers and—

Knock. Knock.

Who banged on his door at this hour?

He shoved his chair back and pulled the string to tighten his pajama bottoms. Where had he thrown his robe?

Knock. Knock. Louder this time.

"Hang on. I'm coming!" He glanced around the new cottage. No robe in the kitchen to throw over his p.j.'s. He hurried through the living room. No robe. He stuck his head into both bedrooms. Clothes scattered haphazardly on the bed and over the floor, ah, there was his robe.

The pounding increased. He tied on his robe.

Enough racket to wake the dead. He opened the door.

****

Gloria stepped back.

The man looked a mess. His deep-blue lapis eyes were shot with red. Had he just returned from an all-night binge at Sam's?

His dark hair stood on end like a scared bootlegger left holding the bag. All in all he looked like he'd been out on an all-night toot.

She should come back later. This was obviously a bad time.

"You?"

"Good morning." She'd get nowhere if he figured out what she truly thought of men who got drunk. Could she handle working with another? What choice did she have? "Yep. It's me."

Buzz always cautioned she could catch more flies with honey than with vinegar. "I just stopped by to offer my mechanic services. I caught your show yesterday and noticed your engine ran a little rough. I'm pretty good with engines." She pasted on her sweetest smile. His engine wasn't the only thing running rough.

His mouth dropped open.

She forced her gaze away from his lips. Had to be the most faultless ones she'd encountered. Or they would be if he shut his mouth.

"Your carb needs adjusting." Just like his attitude. "I brought over my tool box." She fluttered her lashes a tiny bit. "I thought lending a hand might be the neighborly thing to do."

He slammed his mouth shut, and his eyes gave her the once over like Charlie Chaplain did to the dancehall girl in *The Gold Rush*. "You ..." His Adam's apple slid up and down his muscular throat. "You repair engines?"

He sure was slow on the uptake. She gazed past him into the spacious bungalow. "Worked on them for years. I can tear an engine down and build it up in less time than it takes to drive from Kitty Hawk to Rodanthe." Okay, maybe she exaggerated, but how could she think with him scowling at her?

He braced both arms against the door jamb as if to keep her out of his bungalow. "I don't believe you."

She bent and pulled her tool box from behind the wooden crate waiting for the morning's milk delivery and hefted the heavy container up with both hands. "See."

Fresh coffee scent wafted from inside. How long since she'd drunk a cup. "Let's talk about how I can help you over a cup of Java."

"You want to come inside?"

She pointed to several metal lawn chairs positioned cozily on the cement under the shady porch roof. "Bring out the coffee, and we can sit on the porch." She placed her toolbox down by the door, bounced over to the nearest chair and plopped down. She'd do almost anything for a cup of Java. Even talk nice to this flat tire.

"Hold on while I get dressed." He ducked back inside the bungalow.

Took him a long time, but when he slammed the front screen door behind him, gone was the wreck. He resembled some lucky gal's dreamboat. Not hers. She'd been on her own long enough to know men weren't to be trusted. Especially ones that were easy on the eyes.

He shoved his hand through his wavy dark hair, still damp from a shower.

Had he showered for her? She grinned. Maybe coming back to badger him hadn't been such a bad idea.

A line still slanted between his dark brows. "You ready for that coffee?"

"I am."

He disappeared back into the bungalow. Soon, he shouldered his way out past the wooden screen door, carrying two cups of steaming coffee on a tray. He held out the offering.

She reached for one of the heavy white mugs, closed her eyes and inhaled. The aroma smelled like ambrosia.

"You take sugar or cream?"

"No, I like it black and hot. Thanks."

As he pulled the other lawn chair over next to her, metal chair legs scraped on cement. "So, you're a neighbor?"

"Just over that sand dune."

"You live in Curt's cottage?"

"I did." She sipped the hot brew and smiled as the liquid slid down to her empty stomach. She had to vacate tonight. "Annie's folks arrive tomorrow to spend several weeks on the beach."

"Yeah. Fine." His bluest of blue eyes skewered her. "You really can't fix an ailing engine, can you?"

She frowned. Why did men think women had no skills? "Actually I can. Besides walking Buzz's wings, I kept his engine purring like a kitten."

"Until a few days ago."

She cringed. Hadn't she beat herself up enough

about that? Even a cup of hot coffee wasn't worth this. She stood and handed the cup to him. "You're a sap, you know." She headed for the steps.

He thrust a long leg out that blocked her exit. "Sorry. You're right. That was a bum thing to say." He heaved a deep breath. "Let's start over. Sit down. I might have an engine I'd like you to work on."

"Really?"

"Yeah. When my head aches, I can't work on my engine." He massaged his temples.

"You have a headache?" Of course he would after that binge.

"A doozie." He gazed at his coffee as if the black liquid might make him ill.

"You've got a show today?"

"I'll be fine by show time. Always am."

"You get headaches a lot?"

"After every show."

"Maybe you should quit flying."

"Maybe I should quit breathing. Same thing." His jaw jutted.

Honey. Remember honey catches more flies. Don't mention his drinking. "Don't I know it. I love the freedom of soaring through the air."

"We agree on something."

She lowered herself back down onto the metal seat and retrieved her coffee. "Look, I need a job bad. Buzz was like a father to me, so he owed me considerable back pay that I can't collect. I'm flat busted."

"I'll pay if you get that engine running smooth."

"That's a drop in the bucket. I need a daily gig." She fluttered her lashes. "And you need more show time. I checked. Your audience is dwindling."

He slumped in the chair and took a long, slow gulp of coffee. "You seem to know a lot more about me than I do about you."

"I'm good. I'm really good. I'm surprised you haven't heard of me." She pulled a poster from her only purse, the glass-beaded clutch she'd bought to carry when she'd worked at Sam's Speakeasy, and unfolded the paper. "See."

Her clutch looked odd paired with her coveralls, but he probably didn't know fashion. He probably didn't even notice.

He held out his hand and took the poster. "Great picture of you." He stared at her grasping the special pole affixed to Buzz's Jenny with her right hand and holding her left leg high above her head with her left hand. The bi-plane skimmed close to fields of growing corn, tomato plants, and peach orchards.

"The poster looks recent."

"It is." Cost her a week's grocery money.

He raised dark brows. "You perform acrobatics as well?"

"Like I said yesterday, I do it all. The riskier, the better I like it. The crowds love me."

"You don't look strong enough to withstand the wind."

"I'm all muscle. Not an inch of fat on my body."

"Hard to tell under those coveralls."

Did he have a twinkle in his azure eyes? "I've got a costume. Believe me, I'm strong. I'm fit." She set her coffee mug on the small metal table between them, stepped off the porch into the sand, arched her spine and flipped into a back cartwheel. Then she stood and grasped her left leg with her left hand and touched her toe to her head.

He stared at her as if she were a new kind of plane he'd never flown. "Okay. So you really are the goods." He gulped his coffee as if the caffeine would heal whatever ailed him. "You can put your leg down now."

"So, let's talk money." She stepped back onto the porch, dropped down in the chair and reached for her coffee. She liked it hot.

"Not so fast. I just sank all my funds into buying these fourteen cottages."

"They're the bees knees. I noticed they were all new and shared a common theme with the soft yellow paint. Classy."

"Right. But I don't have a lot of cash. How long is your act?"

"As long as you want it to be." She fluttered her lashes.

His cheeks reddened. "What kind of money was Buzz paying?"

Should she lie? She barely lived from week to week on what Buzz gave her? "What do you think increasing your revenue by at least seventy-five percent would be worth to you?" She tilted her head and gazed up at him with that look she'd been told knocked men on their heels.

He swallowed. "I don't know."

"I'm sure we can come to an agreement."

He heaved himself off the chair, a frown on his face. "Um, there's one other thing you need to know. This might be a deal-breaker."

"Give it to me."

He was her last option. Her heart stuttered. Vincent made certain none of the other pilots would let her near their planes. But if Maitland had a drinking problem, she'd buy a gun to protect herself and work for Sam.

Chapter 3

Rand frowned and pinched the bridge of his nose. "I only have three more shows booked."

"That's no problem. Buzz and I had twenty shows lined up. I can get us more."

"It's not that simple. I take time off periodically to practice navigation and long distance flying. I'm going to fly across the Atlantic to set the world record. I'll be the first man to fly from New York City to Paris, France." Rand paced the porch and allowed the flame of his enthusiasm to fire up. "I'll be the first man in history to dine in New York one day and the next day I'll lounge at a Paris café." He beamed. "My name will appear in history books." He made a wry face. "I only barnstorm to keep me in cash."

"Wow." She took a sip of coffee. "That's ambitious." She gazed out to the Atlantic, just starting to sparkle as the fog cleared. “But we can work our shows around your schedule. I’m certain we can.”

She was sure single-minded. Banking on the determined way she spoke, maybe they could.

Should he tell her the real dilemma? No. Not now. Not ever. He rubbed the back of his neck. “What’s your angle?”

She tilted her chin down and gazed up with wide eyes, her lips slightly puckered.

Blast, she was pretty. When she gave him that look his knees went weak.

“As soon as we advertise my act, you’ll have producers flocking to you like birds to a feather gala.” She thrust her fingers through the straps on the bib of her overalls. “They’ll clamor for more shows than you can fly. But we’ll schedule time for your long-distance practice trips.”

Did he really have time to work in more barnstorming shows? With his real estate business ended in Wilmington, maybe he did.

But could she wing walk? She did have the compact body of an acrobat—what he could see of it hidden in those oversize overalls and white shirt. In a fitted costume, she’d have audiences eating out of her dainty little hand. With that bouncy blonde hair and those startling gray eyes, she’d look like a fairy on his wing. ‘Course they couldn’t see her eyes behind goggles in the air, but the posters and flyers would show her attributes. People would fall in love with her. She would be the darling of Kitty Hawk.

He cleared his throat. He was such a dope, already planning his schedule around her. But she wasn't the problem. "I don't think what you have in mind can work out."

"Why not?" Her gray eyes turned from feathery doves to gunmetal steel. "Why on earth not?" She scooted forward in her chair and slapped her hands on her hips. "Give me one good reason."

The change in her toppled him off-balance. Out of his element. At a disadvantage.

He frowned. He had more than one reason. Matter-of-fact he had three whoppers. "Okay. Say I wanted you to walk my wing. I can't pay you more than twelve dollars a week." His voice sounded sharp. What was wrong with him?

The hope slid off her face.

His chest contracted. A new knot formed over the ones already twisting his stomach. "Or at least I couldn't pay you much more." That woe-be-gone expression hit him harder than the steely-eyed one.

"What's not much more?"

He set his empty coffee cup on the table. "Fifteen bucks a week." He clinched his fists. Where would he find fifteen extra bucks a week? He'd upped his bid because that hopelessness on her face brought him to his knees.

"Oh."

"And I've no money for advertising."

A slender finger rubbed her chin. "That's your

best offer?" The dark pupils in her beautiful eyes dilated.

He could almost see her brain churning.

"You said you own all these cottages?" She gestured to his empty money suckers.

"Yep. My money's tied up in those two bedroom, one bath bungalows." What he had left of the jack he'd earned during the war. He would not ask Dad for help. The old man thought him a goof-off and would never finance any flying scheme. Dad lived and breathed investing in Band-Aids and Q-Tips. Of all the great new inventions, Dad backed the most boring.

She heaved a sigh, and her slender shoulders slumped. Then she grinned. "How about throwing in one of those shacks rent-free?"

He nodded. Man, she had him eating out of her hand. Her happy expression made him willing to do anything she asked. No one else had ever gotten away with that.

"Are you a fisherman?"

"I go out occasionally."

"Throw in a fish or two, three times a week, and we've got a deal." She stood and stretched out her hand.

Those big, gray eyes could mesmerize a monkey. What had she said about a deal? "Sorry. What did you say?"

"Fifteen dollars and a rent-free cabin buys you a world-renowned wing-walker." She thrust out a small hand. "Shake on it. I'll move in this afternoon."

His mouth hung open. He snapped it closed. She had his hand in a grasp and pumped his arm up and down.

"Which one is mine?"

"Umm.

They're all vacant." His F*or Rent* signs waited in the kitchen. Blank boards that needed printing and painting by some hand more artistic than his.

"Then I'll take the one next to yours. The view is magnificent. "

He shook his head. Somehow her sunshine and optimism lessened his headache. "Isn't this afternoon a little soon for you?"

"I'm ready to move in and to fly. Want to rehearse this afternoon after your show?"

"Um. I'm tied up after the show." He'd be down and out with the headache. "But I'll help you move now. You're just down the beach in Curt's cottage?"

"I don't need any help. I'll have my things inside that new cottage by ten o'clock." For the first time she looked a little unsure of herself. "It is furnished isn't it?"

"Sure. Down to the pots and pans in the kitchen." He grabbed a deep breath. "Go on inside and look around. It's not locked."

"That's okay. I'll just get my stuff and move in." Gloria set her empty coffee cup on the tiny table, leaped to her feet and gathered up her toolbox. With a toss of those blonde curls and a cheerful wave, she scampered down the steps and out the picket fence gate.

Was she afraid if she stayed he'd renege the offer she'd bewitched out of him?

Even clad in overalls and some kind of boots with her bobbed hair flying in the wind, Gloria Richards made watching worthwhile as she scooted down the beach toward Curt's cottage.

Rand rubbed his chin. What just happened? She steamrolled right over him and now she would move in next door? He shook his head. How did that happen?

He slouched back down into the metal porch chair. What would that ray of sunshine and dynamo of a woman think if she knew his secrets? She wouldn't be so eager to join his act.

Would she be safe flying with him? The twists in his stomach tightened.

His coffee had grown cold, but he gulped the bitter liquid.

What had Curt said about his little moocher? Rand rubbed the back of his neck. Then he remembered.

'She's trouble. She's a jinx. She walks your wing, you die.'

****

Gloria waltzed into Curt's cottage. She shook her head.

Maitland considered only three booked shows

a deal-breaker? What was his problem? She and Buzz had plenty of shows lined up. But she'd have to keep a keen eye out to see if the fly boy drank. And she'd get a key to her cottage. Thanks to Sam and Vincent she'd learned to lock her door at night.

Her little gold and white puppy wriggled all over her body in welcome.

She knelt to pet Daisy. "I'll contact those producers and let them know of the change in pilots. They'll be delighted to discover they don't have to hustle out and schedule new shows."

She slid down past the edge of the couch and sat cross-legged on the cool linoleum floor. Her warm puppy hopped onto her lap and licked her face.

"Daisy, something tells me the high and mighty Rand Maitland is hiding some vital information from us."

Daisy tilted her head and smiled. Her long tongue lolled out the side of her mouth.

"Something important." She frowned. "Did he feed me a bunch of hokum about not having enough money himself in order to pay me less?" She scratched the back of Daisy's floppy ears. "Everyone knows he comes from money. And what was that transformation from frog to dreamboat with one shower?"

She leaned back against the couch leg and stared sightlessly at the wall of the bungalow.

Daisy snuggled in her lap and lay her head over Gloria's arm.

"He looked terrible when he opened the door, but ten minutes later when he brought the coffee out to the porch he looked fresh." Gloria gazed down at her baggy dungarees. "I never saw a hang-over beaten that quickly."

She held Daisy's silken head in both hands and gazed into her adoring brown eyes, then she touched her forehead to the sweet dog. "I bet Maitland's not more than five years older than I am. Whatever made me think he was an older man?" She sighed. "Hope, I guess. Well, I won't let him get close enough to amass any ideas. Our contacts will be strictly business."

She straightened and let Daisy's head sink onto her knee. "Maybe that article in the newspaper calling him a hero pilot of the Great War made me think he was older." She twisted her lips into a wry smile. "I wish he was. I don't like working with a man that young." She sighed so long and so deep that Daisy raised her head to lick her face.

"But I don't have a choice, do I?"

Daisy thumped her tail on the floor.

"What's his secret?"

More tail thumping.

Gloria jumped to her feet. She had to pack. She needed to move into that bungalow before the man changed his mind.

She sailed into the bedroom, Daisy's cool nose tickling her bare ankle.

"Wait until you see our new home. The bungalows Maitland owns are the elephant's eyebrows. We'll have two whole bedrooms and a bath with a tub." She gave a little skip and opened the closet door.

"Our new living room has a nifty view of the Atlantic. And there's a table and chairs in a bay window nook beside the kitchen. I haven't seen much of the inside yet, just peeked over Maitland's shoulder, but I'm certain the cottage is the swankiest place we've ever lived in."

She gazed down into Daisy's large, brown, adoring puppy-dog eyes. "If you have an accident while I'm out wing-walking, the mess won't hurt the floor a speck." She swept the shaggy blonde bundle up in her arms and danced around the tiny bedroom. "You'll love living there."

She flopped Daisy down on the unmade bed. Rand Maitland didn't wear a wedding ring. That meant trouble. Nothing but trouble. Her throat tightened. Why did Buzz have to leave her?

"You weren't even born when I had my first bad experience with a pilot." She shook her head. She'd vowed never again to work for a young man. "Safety lies in age." But there weren't many older stunt pilots. She scratched behind Daisy's ears. "I guess men lose their gusto for risk as they mature."

Pulling the case from the pillow, she raced back to the closet. She peeled her white dress from the hanger, snagged her red high heels with two fingers and laid them all on the bed. She opened the top drawer of the battered chest, scooped up her trousers, her other pair of coveralls, and two shirts from the drawer. Then she carefully folded her clothes with the white dress on top and slipped them inside the pillow case. After rummaging in the back of the closet, she pulled out a paper bag and packed her one pair of sandals, red heels, and black wing-walking shoes in the bag. From the bottom dresser drawer, she drew out her trade-mark black fitted tights and folded them over the dress inside the pillowcase, then packed her flight cap on top.

"I'll come back for you and my underwear. I won't be long." She smiled and nodded at Daisy.

The little darling clicked, clicked, clicked beside her to the door. She'd have to trim her nails. Cradling the pillowcase in both hands, she maneuvered the screen door open. "See you in a few minutes."

Daisy hung her head.

Less than five minutes later, sand drifting into her short work boots, she opened the door to Cottage Number Two.

Gasp.

Real black and white tiles on the floor sparkled brand-spanking new. Never walked on. She wedged off her sand-covered boots and left them on the porch. Then she tiptoed through the dream cottage.

The kitchen nook looked so cozy. She could cook scrumptious meals here. And the view through the crisp white-curtained window displayed the best ocean crashing on the sand scene she'd ever laid eyes on. She stood watching blue waves roll in to froth white on the light sand. Turning from the window, her imagination placed a blue checkered tablecloth on the table and a vase of the local water violets in the center. She could hardly wait to cook on the new-fangled gas cook stove and store food in her new-model Frigidaire Electric Refrigerator. She swung the door wide.

"Oh, my." She tugged open a tiny freezer area. "This is no ice box!" She slid down into the splits right in the middle of the tiled floor. "Wait 'til Daisy gets a load of this!" She muscled her legs together and stood. "If anyone saw me, they'd think I was crazy." She giggled. "But I'm so happy! And I gotta stay flexible for my new job."

Clothes carefully placed on an aqua cushion, she plunked down on the new rattan couch and stretched her feet on the overstuffed footstool. A small rattan coffee table and a rattan chair fairly begged her to invite friends in. Maybe when Annie returned from Europe she would come to visit.

She swept up her clothes and danced a jig to the bedrooms.

She chose the bedroom facing east so the sun could splash her face with glory every morning, and she wouldn't oversleep. After hanging her clothes in the closet, she arranged her shoes in a neat row beneath. Fortunately, Rand had provided hangers.

"There!" She had only to leash Daisy and jam her unmentionables into the pillowcase, and she had moved out of Curt's cottage.

She pulled in a deep, happy breath. "Ain't we got fun!" she belted. This time she meant the words. This morning's sorrow eased to lighthearted joy.

She had a job. She had a home. And what a home! She had her dog. What more could she want?

Nothing could go wrong now.

Chapter 4

Rand knocked on the door of Cottage Number Two. He would ask her straight out about the jinx thing. Not that he believed in that superstition. But he'd seen strange things happen during the war when buddies left for a mission without their lucky talisman. Too many hadn't returned. So maybe he *was* a little superstitious. Just how many pilots besides Buzz had she'd worked with who died?

The door opened. Her misty gray eyes blinked, and her slender hand fluttered to her throat.

Was she fearful? Or had he startled her?

"Hi. Thought I would look in and see if you needed more help moving than you thought you might." Lame excuse. He'd watched her from behind his front window curtains as she'd made the two trips with her pillow case and dog. He'd frowned at the dog. His unpainted signs all would state N*o pets.*

But what could a dog hurt? Already he bent rules for her. That had to stop! She tugged too much at his crazy heart and sent him into protective mode.

"No thank you. I'm just fine. All moved in." She edged the door shut.

He put his foot in the way. "If you need anything, just stick your head out the door and holler."

"I'm fine. I'm sure I won't need a thing."

The door pressed against his foot. "Those fish you wanted. Would tomorrow be too soon for you?" Going fishing? Was he unhinged? He had to get that motor running.

Her whole face brightened. The door eased open. "Really? Tomorrow would be wonderful."

"Umm, would you like to go with me?" Chump! Taking a woman fishing was plain dumb.

Her eyes widened. A frown flitted across her forehead. The smile she offered looked polite. "Oh, no thank you."

"You don't fish. I'd be glad to show—"

"I used to fish before...never mind." She offered a rueful, little smile. "I don't have time right now." She turned to gaze back inside the bungalow. "I've got to...you know...get settled."

"Right." How much settling did she have to do? The place had everything, including towels and bed clothes. That was the whole idea for vacation renters. "So, about my engine. Think you could give it a look this morning? I have a show this afternoon."

Her whole face lit up. "Of course you do. We could rehearse this afternoon after your show, I—"

"No!" Blast he hadn't meant to raise his voice.

Her gray eyes grew as angry as a hurricane blowing in. "I *am* your wing-walker."

"Of course you are." Phew, what a fire cracker! "But my audience isn't expecting you. I'll tell my producers today, and they'll pencil you in for the final two shows."

She slapped her hands on her hips and wagged her finger at him. "You'll do more than pencil me in." She bit her lip and the tempest disappeared as fast as it had arisen. "Sorry, with you I forget honey is better than vinegar."

What the Sam Hill was she talking about? He ran a hand through his hair.

She widened those gorgeous smoky eyes and peeked up at him with a sidewise glance.

His insides softened into airplane goo.

"My producers will contact you with times and dates for our upcoming shows."

"Yeah. Yeah. Okay. Thanks. Will do." He was babbling. He pulled his foot off the threshold.

"I could fix your engine after lunch. It would be lovely and save us both time, if you brought a bite out to your Jenny, and we could eat while I take a look to pinpoint the problem."

He glanced at his watch. Eleven. "Sure. Sure. I'll meet you at *The Jazzman* right around noon."

"See you there." She closed the door.

He turned and strode down the short sidewalk, hopped the picket fence, and bee-lined to his front door. He'd have to hit the market down the street for some bread. He'd have to slice the loaf as well as carve the ham he'd cooked yesterday. But how could eating at the plane save time?

He rubbed his clean-shaven jaw. Women. For the life of him, he couldn't figure them out. He'd have no time to catch fish tomorrow. He'd be wiped out after the show. What made him promise fish tomorrow? He was putty in that woman's hands. But what employee asked for fish? She must be strapped for cash. Blast his protective urges.

He stuck his fingers into his pocket and pulled out his cash. Six lousy bucks. Good thing Dad expected him at the house tonight for dinner. He heaved a huge sigh. No doubt Dorothy Courtland would sit at his right again. And he'd have to wear his tux. And be polite to the debutante.

Bother! As if he didn't know these intimate family dinners were created for him. Each week Dad applied more pressure. Sure, Dorothy was a lovely woman. Any fella would be happy to marry her even though she was a total bluenose. But a wife squeezed the life out of a man. Tamed him. Grounded him. Made sure he didn't love a risky job. Kept him from achieving his goals.

Nobody would stop him from setting the world record. Nobody. Especially not a woman.

****

Gloria settled on the spread-out tablecloth in the shadow of *The Jazzman* and removed the wax paper from her sandwich. Her stomach rumbled. She bowed her head. Peeking up through her lashes she grimaced at the astonished look on Maitland's face. She closed her eyes and silently gave thanks for the food.

She didn't care what he thought of her. He was bread and butter. A place to live. A chance to fly. No doubt to some girls he represented the cat's pajamas. But definitely not to her. Men couldn't be trusted. Chivalry had died. Just because she had no family to protect her, men considered her fair game. Easy prey. If Buzz hadn't rescued her that night at Sam's Speakeasy, she'd be dead somewhere lying in a gutter.

She bit into her sandwich. Ham. Not her favorite, but the half sandwich disappeared before she thought again. Well, so what. Her stomach had been grumbling. She didn't need for him to hear the growling.

Maitland poured them both a paper Dixie cup of milk.

She reached for hers and drank half before she took a breath. "Thanks, this hits the spot."

He gazed at her with startled eyes.

They really were the bluest ones she'd ever looked into. Annie's Curt had blue eyes too. They evidently ran in the Maitland family. Blue as the

Caribbean. But his could turn hard, more like agates than seawater. Yet for some reason when he stared at her, which he did a lot, his eyes didn't make her squirm. Men staring at her usually made her uneasy.

She started in on the other half of her sandwich. "This is all you brought?"

He quirked a brow. "I didn't think a little thing like you ate much."

Humph. She'd have to save some to take home to Daisy. This sandwich would have to do until he brought the fish tomorrow. "I'm not so little."

He bit into his sandwich.

She wrapped the rest of the sandwich back in the waxed paper and slid the package into her overalls pocket. She finished the milk and stood. "I'll check that engine now. Would you start her up?"

He jumped up so fast the wax paper from his sandwich fluttered to the sand. Wind caught the crumpled square and blew the paper inland away from the scattered houses on stilts, toward the long row of striking yellow bungalows Maitland owned.

He pretended not to have any money, but he owned all those cottages. He had to be rich. If only he'd be straight with her. She just wanted what she earned. Nothing more. Did he think she was a gold-digger? Did he think with his big blue eyes and dimples he was irresistible? Oh, Buzz, why did you have to go and die? I miss you so.

Rand clanged open the engine cowling and gazed over his shoulder at her.

She'd make certain Maitland never learned about her being alone in the world. She knew about rich men. Not a decent man among them. They looked down at a girl like her who made her own way in life and figured they had a right to take advantage. She wasn't having any more of that. Not on your life.

She frowned harder. Rich men were sly. They invited, 'Come to my party and make it sparkle.' Oh no, they didn't mean enjoy yourself. They meant, let me enjoy you. Nope. They could keep their money and their parties and their beautiful houses. She wouldn't pay the price to enjoy them. Never again.

His dark brows shot up. "What's wrong? You look mad enough to spit worms. Didn't you like the sandwich?"

Gloria gazed down at her clinched hands, smoothed her expression, forced a smile and gave him the sideways glance that always seem to put longing in a man's eyes. "The sandwich tasted good. Now, let's take a look at that engine."

When he climbed up on the wing, the plane tilted slightly under his weight. He thrust a long leg over the fuselage, scooted down into the bucket seat, and turned on the engine.

The sandwich had stopped the gnawing in her stomach, but she wouldn't get paid for another week. What would she and Daisy eat between now and then?

Chapter 5

Three solid raps on her door.

Moonlight filtered into her open window. Who would knock this late? Had to be almost eight. Gloria peeked out the window. Maitland.

Padding barefoot to the door, she slid it open an inch. “Yes?”

“I brought your fish.”

“Wow! This is way over wonderful! An answer to prayer.” She threw open the door.

He walked inside. Lamplight bathed him with a pale glow that threw a giant shadow on the smooth wall.

Her jaw dropped.

He wore a fitted black tux with tails. His white shirt radiated brilliance in the light. He looked high-hat all the way. That the man had Jack and plenty of it screamed out all over him. He was Joe Brooks in person.

"You look spiffy." She crossed her arms over her bib overalls.

"Thanks, I guess. You'd don't seem to like spiffy."

"Don't I? Imagine that?"

A frown flashed across his face and then cleared. He held out a package. "I brought your fish."

She took the butcher-paper wrapped parcel. Her fingers explored the lumps. Had to be at least four pieces inside. They'd keep a couple days in the electric refrigerator. "Did you clean them?"

"What?"

"The fish. Did you clean them?"

"Ugh. No. I bought them. I won't have time to take out the boat tomorrow." His grin looked sheepish. "Seemed the least I could do since you coaxed that engine to purr like a tiger."

"I told you I would." She gripped the fish tighter. "Okay. Well, thank you."

His dark hair glistened in the soft light. Yet he didn't use as much pomade as most men did, and the light gel left his hair wavy rather than slicked back. Maybe he used some rich kind of oil to make his hair look so good. She pulled in a deep breath. He smelled better than good. More like marvelous. "Appears you have a shindig to attend."

"Yeah. Dinner at my dad's."

"You dress like that to eat at your house?" She couldn't help herself, she'd blurted the words and now looked like a Dumb Dora standing there holding his fish.

"About once a week, Dad throws a dinner party. I'm obliged to attend."

He didn't look happy about that. "Oh, of course. A dinner party." Did he have some unlucky poor girl invited to give him a night of enjoyment in payment for the privilege of eating with the family? He wasn't fooling her. He had money.

"Yes. Compulsory."

"Well, thanks for bringing the fish."

He turned to leave.

She caught his sleeve. "I think ten dollars would be fair for getting your engine purring like a contented cat."

He froze. His back stiffened. His jaw jutted. He slowly turned to her. "We shook on fifteen dollars a week."

She ducked her chin, pouted her lips just a little and widened her eyes. "But I really need the extra ten for fixing your engine."

His Adam's Apple rose above his crisp black tie and then lowered. "A deal's a deal. You get fifteen dollars a week for wing-walking and keeping the engine running smooth." He straightened his tie and flicked some invisible lint off his arm. His jaw jutted.

"Of course." She tilted her chin up and gave him her best smile.

His Adam's Apple made that trip up and down his throat. The expression on his face flickered.

He was going to pay her!

Then his jaw hardened and his shoulders stiffened. He turned to leave.

Nope, he wasn't going to give in this time. "Don't be late to your party." She opened the door for him. So much for getting money to advertise their new partnership. Would he get drunk tonight and be unable to fly tomorrow? A pilot with a drinking problem was dangerous. And he held her life in his hands.

One indication he was drunk, and she would buy that gun and work for Sam. A scared singer was better than a dead wing-walker.

Chapter 6

"How did you like our first show?" Rand lifted Gloria down from the wing of his Jenny and then modified his voice and posture to appear nonchalant as he jerked off his helmet, leaned back on the fuselage and crossed his lanky legs.

"I thought we did okay." Gloria turned her back to him. "Would you mind removing my flight cap. I don't want to mess my hair."

We did okay? Rand worked his big fingers among the hooks at the back of Gloria's costume. "I thought we did a heck of a lot better than acceptable. I thought we were magnificent. We were whacking over-the-top. The audience loved us. And did you see the cheering and waving as we taxied by the stands?"

"Oh, Buzz and I always drew an adoring crowd. And they always rushed us at the show's end." She gazed up at him with a smile that dimmed the sunlight.

Her huge, silvery eyes beamed twinkles of light, and her cupid's bow lips turned up in such a bewitching way he almost forgot the headache thundering in his temples.

"I told you I was a draw. You'll get your money's worth when I walk your wing."

"Speaking of...you *were* stupendous out there. I almost lost control of *The Jazzman* watching you."

"You *watched* me?" A frown chased the light from her face. "You are supposed to keep your focus on the plane's controls. My life depends on your keeping *The Jazzman* flying."

"Easy. Don't get your feathers ruffled. I maintained full control at all times. You think a man can only manage one thing at a time?"

She turned to saunter toward the cottages. "I suppose you think you're the cat's meow of pilots." Pink tinted her cheeks.

He followed her through the sand watching the slender body encased in a black bodysuit, small feet taking dainty steps in black wing-walking shoes. "I don't think. I know." He'd seen stars on the silver screen whose light dimmed in her shadow.

She turned and gave him a saucy smile. "I'll give it to you, you're a nifty pilot. But I'd prefer you kept your eyes on your dials while I'm performing. The slightest dip at the wrong time and I'll lose balance and control."

"Trust me. I'll keep a firm foundation beneath your feet...or foot for that matter. That stunt where you touch your foot to the back of your head is—"

"You're making me nervous. How long did you watch?"

"And the one where you hold on by your teeth had my nerves on edge. How can someone so..." he'd almost blurted beautiful, "...small be so strong?"

"Practice." She stopped so suddenly her shoes dug into the sand. "We need to work on that spin where I drop the ladder and hang by my teeth. It was almost too fast. Let's do a practice flight—"

"Not now!"

"Okay, don't bite my head off."

"Sorry." That splitting headache had crashed into him the moment he landed. And he had no extra money for gas to practice with. He had to find something stronger than those new Bayer Aspirins. And rake up some money somewhere. Maybe he could sell his golf clubs.

He sped past her, his boots spitting sand in his wake.

"You got a hot date or something?"

Her breathless laughter followed him to his bungalow door. He called over his shoulder, "Nope, just business. I'll see you tomorrow before the show."

****

Wow, he couldn't wait to get away. Gloria waved at some fans who'd followed them all the way down the sand to the cabins. She paused at the picket fence and signed some autographs.

One tall man waited patiently until she'd autographed for the families, and then stepped forward. "I'd love to take you out for dinner tonight. The Blue Crab is right across the bay. I could pick you up at seven."

Gloria signed her name with a flourish and handed him his program. Normally she didn't date. But she'd eaten the last of Rand's fish yesterday for dinner. All the whole day stretched out in front of her with nothing to do and nothing to eat. She and Buzz had usually puzzled over her program after each show and discussed what could be improved. Then she and Buzz trotted over to his house to eat lunch with Mattie and the twins.

She gave the man holding his program as if it were a precious relic a thorough look-over. "I don't know you."

"Name's Bill Reed. I'm a local here in Kitty Hawk. Not a pilot. I sell insurance. And I don't usually have the courage to invite a lovely wing-walker out to dinner." He smiled, quite a charming smile. "So I hope you won't disappoint me."

She would never have given a second thought to accepting if her stomach hadn't been howling like a ravenous wolf. But Bill looked harmless with his slicked down hair and nice pin-striped suit. A gentleman. Usually Buzz checked out her dates in the rare event she accepted any. But she couldn't expect Rand to do so. Besides Rand had already gone about his business.

"Come on, what do you say. Just dinner and then I'll have you home by nine."

He had the look of a man who usually got what he wanted. A successful appearance. "I don't normally go out with strangers."

"Of course not. I can see you're a nifty girl. But I want to show you off to my pals at the Blue Crab."

She scuffed her ballerinas in the loose sand.

"Tonight's special is lobster tails."

She'd never tasted lobster tails. And he did have a nice smile. "I'd love to." The words popped out of her mouth before she could stop them.

"Swell. I'll pick you up at seven. You live there in cottage two of the Maitland Manors, right?" He nodded toward her cabin.

How did he know? Maybe she'd better not—

"It's okay. Some of the fellas were teasing your pilot until he confessed where you live. He was tight-mouthed at first, but he lost the wager and had to pay up."

A place inside her hollowed out and filled with regret. She gave Bill a granite smile. "Rand lost a wager about me?"

"Not exactly."

"What exactly?"

"The guys baited him into putting his Jenny up against a final pool shot. He lost."

"And how did my name come up?"

“None of us can fly.” Bill hung his head, but flashed her a smile. “We all really wanted to know your name and where you live. We didn’t want the plane.”

“So he traded keeping his Jenny for telling you where I live?” What was Rand doing gambling? So, Rand was a gambler as well as a drinker. Better to know now...why she didn’t take time to fathom.

“Yep. We got the best of the deal. And I won the honor of asking you out first.” His grin was infectious. “I hope you don’t mind. You’re the bee’s knees, and all of fellas would be honored to take you to dinner...and maybe a dance later...if you liked one of us.”

Anger filled the empty place in her heart. Rand traded her privacy for his plane! Drinking and gambling! If the man wasn’t an ace pilot and providing her with a place to live and money to live on, she’d drop him cold.

Bill grinned again. “See you tonight!”

“Yes, tonight.” She turned and continued up the new sidewalk to cottage number two. Tonight at least she’d have a good dinner. Bill appeared to be a good egg. Certainly, having dinner with him one time would be okay. Then perhaps another of the gang he hung with would ask her out for dinner. She’d accept their dinner offers, one per each man. But no dance. And no repeat dates. She didn’t trust even harmless-looking guys.

And she’d give Mr. Rand Maitland an ear full.

Chapter 7

Rand relaxed on his front porch and eyed the flivver pulling up with a squeal of tires on sprays of sand in front of Gloria's cottage. Lights shone from all her windows, and a radio played jazz from where he knew she had her bedroom.

He rubbed a hand through his hair. So, the hot-shots at the country club hadn't wasted any time hustling to his wing-walker.

A tall man, dressed in blazer and slacks, sophisticated enough to show his money, hopped out of the late model Packard limousine. He smoothed his hand through his slicked-back hair and strutted up the porch stairs to the cottage. He glanced over and nodded at Rand.

Rand frowned. The pain in his temples intensified and worked its ache down his neck and into his shoulders where it should have stopped, but somehow sneaked lower into his stomach. The dinner Mom had brought over threatened to upsurge and spill out.

Of course, Bill Reed would be the one who high-handed first dibs on Gloria. The man's family had enough money to ruin Maitland Corporation's investment in Band Aids and Q-Tips. Bill's threat hadn't even been veiled. He'd out-and-out declared he'd ruin Dad if Rand didn't spill the beans about where his wing-walker lived.

Bill's rap on the cottage door sounded possessive. Rand frowned. Bill always got what Bill wanted. Rand massaged the tight muscles at the back of his neck. And Bill always wanted what Rand had. Bill owned two barn-storming planes that were newer and faster than Rand's, but Bill didn't have the guts to fly either of them.

The door opened and Gloria stood silhouetted in the light. Rand pulled in a shaky breath. She wore the same white slinky dress that swirled around her perfect figure the first day she'd approached and asked for a job. Her blonde bob glowed in the backlight. He swallowed hard. She'd looked lovely in the bright sunlight, but she appeared effervescent sandwiched between the living room's backlighting and the moonlight bathing her porch.

Bully Bill leaned in and shoved his face close to her hair.

Rand half-rose from his chair. What the heck was Bill doing? Ha, Gloria didn't like his pushing in that close. She backed away.

"Come on, baby. You're the cat's meow! I hit the jackpot tonight." He grabbed for her hand. "Let's hit the road." Bill's baritone floated clearly to Rand's eavesdropping ears.

The melody of Gloria's voice carried across the white picket fence to where Rand sat rigid in the lawn chair, but he couldn't make out what she said.

"I thought we'd drive over to Sam's Speakeasy and eat in his private dining room." Bill had his hand in the small of Gloria's back and was leading her down the sidewalk to where his Limo waited.

Again, Rand couldn't hear Gloria's reply.

"Nifty. If you'd rather eat at the Blue Crab, your wish is my command." Bill opened the car's door and helped Gloria slide into the luxurious leather front seat.

Rand pulled in a breath. No dancing for Gloria. He leaned forward in the lawn chair and just made out what Bill was saying.

"...hotsy-totsy. We can go to Sam's later." Bill strolled around the limo, opened the door, and slid behind the driver's seat. With a squeal of tires which jack-knifed the rear of the car, he took off.

Night closed in on Rand as if Gloria had been a glowing ray of moonlight, but the moon had set. He slumped in the lawn chair, his legs splayed in front. This morning he'd had a fairy dynamo displaying unbelievable acrobatics on his wing, and tonight that nymph left with another man. And Bill Reed was not a man to accept *no* from a lady. He was a formidable adversary.

Rand leaped from the chair, slammed the screen behind him, sped into his bedroom, rustled in his bureau drawer, and grabbed his car keys. He'd keep an eye on Gloria to make certain Bill didn't take any liberties with her.

Why had she accepted him anyway? She hadn't seemed to be a flirty type of girl. Why would she date the first fella who....?

Blast and blast! The girl didn't have any food in her house. She accepted Bill because she was hungry. Rand slammed the bureau drawer shut. Confound his empty pockets.

Like it as much as he'd like to pet a tiger, he'd have to bend his pride and ask Dad for a loan. He couldn't tolerate Gloria dating men just to have something to eat.

He glanced out his bedroom window at the dark bungalow next door. Why hadn't Dorothy Courtland stirred up even one iota of what he felt for Gloria?

He switched off his bedroom light. Oh, dear God. Had he committed the fatal mistake? Was he in a nosedive toward a horrible crash? Had he fallen in love with Gloria?

Rand wiped sweat off his brow and chased out to his car. Whatever his problem, he'd keep watch on the Blue Crab and ensure that Gloria got home safely. He didn't trust Bill Reed.

No, he couldn't be in love. He simply had to protect his new act.

No way he could be in love. Not him.

Not now. Falling for Gloria was too inconvenient. Too costly. Too impossible. And way too painful.

Chapter 8

Gloria slammed the cottage door in Bill's face. Had fighting the man's advances off all evening been worth the tummy-filling lobster dinner? She twisted the dead bolt. "Go away!" She hoped her scream didn't wake her next-door neighbor. She glanced out her window at the dark cottage. She sure wouldn't want to wake Rand if he slept off a binge.

"Aw, come on, Gloria. I'll be good. Just give me a chance, you'll see." Muffled by the door, Bill's cultured tone belied his words.

"Don't call me and don't come back." Gloria commanded through the sturdy wooden door.

Daisy barked and barked, running in frantic circles at her feet.

"Good girl, Daisy." Gloria switched off her living room light and stood in the darkness to emphasize her point. She'd known better than to accept a date with a rich fella. One and all, they took advantage. As if she didn't know they would only marry one of their own set. Rich fellas never married girls who worked for a living. Not that she wanted a husband, but she had wanted the man to respect her.

Nope, she'd accept no more dates. Even as she quenched her appetite with the rich food, Bill had kept his eyes jumping all over her like frogs hopping on lily pads. Almost made her lose her appetite. She'd try her hand at fishing on the pier instead.

She gazed out her bedroom window at the moonlight shimmering on the sand and transforming the sea into floating stars. She slipped off her red spiked heels. She could stay here forever and be perfectly content. Slipping carefully out of her dress, her thoughts wondered over to the pilot next door. Considering his overalls and grease-coated hands, and that he barnstormed for a living, he didn't appear rich. But he did own fourteen cottages he could rent for a tidy sum. And his older brother and Annie lived in quite a beautiful house on stilts on the Outer Banks.

But Rand hadn't made any passes. Rather he'd almost run from her after their show this morning. Thank goodness, he wasn't interested in her. Well, if the pilot stayed sober and kept his end of their business deal, she would ask no more of him.

And happily he asked no more of her! That

thought smoothed the frown from her forehead.

She headed out to her kitchen. “Come here, Daisy. I brought you some lobster.”

A light flickered on in Rand’s kitchen.

Had he just returned from somewhere? She could have sworn she’d seen him lounging on his porch when she left with Bill for the Blue Crab. Had Rand waited for her to leave and then gone out to drink? Well, he’d have a whole day to sober-up before their next show. She’d keep an eye on him tomorrow night to make certain he didn’t slip out on to his favorite watering hole.

Rand could have been a real heart-throb if he hadn’t been a drinker. If they hadn’t been bloodshot, those lapis-lazuli eyes of his could lodge right inside a girl’s heart.

****

Gloria swung her purse and sang *‘Ain’t Misbehavin, No one to talk to, All by myself…’*

Life was good. Mattie and the twins were doing okay. She’d had a hard time tearing herself away, but now she needed to find a pole and some string and catch her dinner.

Even with food so hard to come by, life was good. The twins looked forward to school in a few weeks, and Mattie had found a job cooking for the Gallagher Restaurant. Not a job Gloria wanted. She had no talent for cooking. *Thank you, Father God, for my job. You know how I love the thrill of soaring above an adoring crowd with the wind in my face and a steady wing beneath my ballerinas. We all miss Buzz, but You are taking care of us.*

"You're perky today. Have a good date last night?"

Gloria jumped, so startled she almost tumbled to the sidewalk. "Ow. Where did you come from?"

Rand put a helping hand on her elbow. "Sorry, I didn't mean to surprise you."

"Guess I was in my own little world." She glanced up at him so appealing in his white dress shirt, open at the collar and emphasizing his broad shoulders. Any other girl would capture him for her dreamboat. She slowed her steps and leaned closer to smell his breath. Umm, nice. Minty. No hint of liquor. "You're all dressed up. Been someplace special?"

"Putting an ad in the paper to rent the cottages." He cleared his throat. "So how was the date last night?"

Why did he care? "So, so. The Blue Crab serves a great lobster."

"Yeah, speaking of...I overbought groceries this morning. The seafood will go bad before I can use it all. Want some?"

Did she ever! "Depends on what kind." She kept her voice cool, not too eager.

"Shrimp, sole, and a few lobsters. But they're still alive. Know how to boil a lobster?"

She didn't, but the library was within walking distance. "Sure, I could use all your excess seafood.

Why did you buy so much? Having a party?"

"Um, no, just got carried away at the fisherman's wharf." He gazed up the sidewalk to her cottage. "Here we are. Shall I bring them over now?"

"Sure. Now's as good a time as any." She couldn't wait to get her hands on that food. What kind of man bought too much seafood?

"I also got my hands on some fresh clams. Thought we might have a clambake. Just you and me, and Daisy, of course. Sort of a beach party..." His cheeks tinted to a ruddy shade. "... for attracting renters."

She loved clams better than anything. "You mean eat outdoors on the beach?"

"Sure. In front of the cottages. We'll have a bonfire and people walking by can see how cozy these cottages will be to rent. With parties thrown in for good measure."

"Just you and me?"

"You could invite some friends if you want."

She'd never had time to make friends. "But we need to get to sleep early so we can be ready for tomorrow's show. Probably best not to invite anyone who would stay late."

"Okay. Say around six?"

What was that warning strumming in her brain? Warning her against the swoosh and whirl of attraction. Warning her to stay away from Rand? And yet, if he was with her, he wouldn't be out drinking. "Okay, six then."

She'd wear the clean coveralls. No one could think her the least bit alluring swallowed in denim.

She'd ask him about his drinking and gambling.

Chapter 9

Rand filled the deep kettle with half water and half beer and lugged it out on the sand in front of Gloria's cottage. He shoved his hands into the pockets of his casual slacks. What was he doing? Even though this woman shared his love of thrills and danger, she could interfere with his goal of setting the long distance flying record before Charlie Lindbergh. He had no place in his life for a woman. He had to prove to Dad that he could make sufficient money to finance his own way without joining Dad's investment company.

And here this petite daredevil had already compelled him to bend his knees before Dad to procure a small loan. Something he'd promised himself he'd never do.

He built a fire and set the kettle on to boil.

Last night Dad had been cordial when he'd told

him he wasn't interested in getting engaged to Dorothy, nor would he ever be. Maybe Dad was coming around to his viewpoint. He ran his fingers through his hair and frowned. Unfortunately, he'd slipped up and mentioned Gloria's name once or twice during the evening, and Dad had given him that look.

Humph, no way he was romantically interested in Gloria. But let Dad think so if he wanted. Would keep him from shoving another debutante down his throat.

Gloria walked out her front door and waved.

She looked lost in the coveralls. But they didn't diminish her elfin beauty at all. In the late afternoon shadows her hair haloed around her heart-shaped face, and her smile rivaled the sun. Why wasn't such a lovely woman married? Maybe she had been. He knew nothing about her.

"How can I help?"

Her throaty voice sent pleasure rippling through his nervous system. He cleared his throat. "You can quarter the potatoes. I peeled them earlier."

"Oh you've got a huge kettle of food here already to throw into the pot. You've got potatoes and corn on the cob and littleneck clams and butter. Cooked chorizo. Fresh onion. All ready to throw into the pot." She clapped her hands and danced on the sand.

"I'll quarter these ears of corn. They cook better in smaller pieces."

"Oh, this is so lovely."

Wow. A man would do almost anything to keep her looking so happy.

She picked up the paring knife and started quartering the shiny, white potatoes.

"You can toss in some bay leaves after I dump in the potatoes, the corn, and the clams. Then they simmer together about twenty minutes until the potatoes are tender and the clams open. I usually use half water and half beer to cook them in." He dumped all the ingredients into the boiling pot. "Now we salt and pepper and wait."

"Oh, the scent is outstanding. The smell alone will bring renters."

He tossed out a blanket on the sand, unpacked the picnic hamper and handed her a couple bowls and silverware, which she spread out, along with the red and white checked napkins.

"What do you like to drink? I have water, ice tea, and lemonade."

"Water is just fine." The lazy sun heading toward the horizon backlit her, tinting her blonde curls rosy.

"Here's the melted butter to dip the clams in and an empty bucket to toss the shells into."

He set out the rolls and butter. "I have damp washcloths for our hands after. So, don't be bashful about digging in."

The sun dipped down toward a fabulous sunset painting the sky with pastel colors, and his insides with quiet contentment.

****

Gloria lay back on her elbows and heaved a deep, contented sigh. She'd eaten enough to keep her for all of tomorrow. And food had never tasted so good. She should ask Rand about his drinking but hated to break the spell of a wonderful late afternoon on the beach.

What was that feeling inside her chest? Happiness! She hadn't felt this happy since.... maybe she'd never before experienced this euphoric joy. Well, yes she had. That night she'd wandered into the tent meeting and heard about receiving forgiveness and a new life. The night she'd asked Jesus into her life, and He'd made her a new creation, and given her a new future. The night all the heaviness of sin had slid away, and she'd become a new person. Yep, that was the last time she'd experienced true happiness.

But this evening was good too. In quite a different way. She lounged on a blanket, alone on a beach with a man. And she knew somehow, deep in her heart, he was a good man. Perhaps even a Christian man. She would not have to fight him off when darkness fell. She actually trusted him. Plus, hide his motives as he tried, he'd prepared this feast for her because somehow he sensed she needed food...at least until payday.

Yes, Rand was a good man. She hated to disillusion herself by asking about his drinking.

She'd rather lie here, listen to the song of the sea as it surged onto the beach, and watch his silhouette against the setting sun as he lounged cross-legged on the far edge of the blanket.

Yet she must. She sat up and faced him. "About your drinking—"

"Drinking?" His back stiffened like a ramrod. "What are you talking about?"

"When you binge and wake up the next day with blood-shot eyes?" She made her voice gentle. Mama said honey makes the words go down easier and sweet takes the sting out of sour.

He started stacking the dirty dishes into the picnic basket. "I don't drink." He slapped the dirty silverware onto the dishes so hard she feared they would break. "And especially I don't drink when I fly." He stared at her. "What gave you that idea?"

"Your headaches. Your blood-shot eyes." Her voice faltered at the deep tones of hurt in his voice.

"Oh." He rested his hands on his thighs and gazed out at the sun sinking below the distant line of the sea. "I guess you have a right to know." He rubbed his hand over his face as if he wanted to forget this discussion. "I told you when I met you that I have good reasons not to take you on as my wing walker."

"Yes, you did," she urged when he fell silent.

"I get a small government pension."

"You were an Army Air Corps pilot." She nodded. "An ace."

"A pilot only gets a pension if he received a

permanent injury." He hunched his head. Shadows hid his expression.

"And."

"My right eye is blind."

She gasped. "And yet you fly loops and –"

"Yep. As long as I fly left, I'm fine."

"And that blind eye makes both your eyes bloodshot at times? I don't understand."

"I have headaches."

"Oh."

"They grow worse when I fly."

"Oh."

"So you don't need to worry about my drinking." His smile looked as cranked on as an unresponsive motor.

She gathered the remainder of the clam bake to put into his picnic basket. "I see."

But should Rand be flying at all? Might he pass out from his headaches? One wobble of the wings and she would slide right off.

And she wore no parachute.

Chapter 10

"I don't believe you." Rand shut his front door in the face of the two men.

"It's true. You best heed our warning." Sam Stevenson, owner of Sam's Speakeasy, stuck a hard hand against the doorframe and leaned in to press his nose against Rand's screen door. "The minx is a jinx. Sure, she'll sweet-talk you and tease you with that innocent come-on she has, but take my word for it, Gloria Richards is bad news. Just ask Buzz Randall." Sam cocked his head and sneered. "Oh, that's right, you can't. Buzz bought the farm because he hired that jinx."

"Better take our word for it, Maitland." The other man Sam had introduced as Vincent Vinnetti twirled his panama straw hat in his hand and tapped his two-toned wingtips to emphasize his words.

Rand straightened his vest. The banging at his front door had awakened him from his after-performance nap. The new medication put an end to his headaches, but left him with a need for an hour's sleep before resuming his work. He smothered a yawn. "So why come to me with this cock-and-bull story of a jinx?"

"She's not only bad luck, she left me in the lurch. I headlined her at my club. She bailed without a word. Left me high and dry for a performer." Sam reached inside his waistcoat and pulled out his pocket watch. He glanced at it, flashing the expensive gold. "We gotta go. Just want to leave a word for the wise." He clapped his derby on his head. "No one in his right mind will hire that missy." He turned to leave.

"Hold on a minute. You say Gloria worked for you? As what?"

"My songbird. Until she flew the coop. Left me high and dry. For no reason."

"So, what's in it for you to come out here to warn me?" Rand's mind snapped into alert. What did these two men, who looked like they stepped out of an ad for mobsters to hire, have to do with Gloria? Did she have a shady background? What did he really know of her?

"She's trouble with a capital T." Sam and Vincent scowled like twin gargoyles. As they pivoted to leave, Sam's suit coat, caught by a stray sea-breeze flew open, revealing a gun inside a holster hanging from his shoulder.

Rand braced a hand against his door jamb and watched the two men strut down his sidewalk and swagger to the Lincoln Town Car parked on the hard sand in front of the cottage, its shiny whitewalls dirtied by loose sand.

How was Gloria mixed up with those two thugs?

****

The luxury car pulled up in front of her bungalow. Gloria had watched the two men get out and talk with Rand. She glanced around the cozy living room. Not even a poker to defend herself with. She rushed barefoot into her bedroom and tugged open the closed door. Nothing.

Perhaps a pot from the kitchen.

Knocks thundered at her front door. She'd left it open to catch the breeze from the ocean. Nothing separated her from the two men but an unlatched screen door. She'd never make it past the front door to the kitchen for the pot. She stooped and grabbed her high-heeled red shoe.

The banging continued.

Should she hide in here or confront them?

The banging stopped, and the screen door thumped shut. Heavy steps thudded against the wooden floor.

They were inside. She wouldn't confront them in the bedroom. Not those two goons. They'd toss her across the bed and....

She rushed out to face them in the living room. "Get out. You have no right to enter my home!" Despite her best effort, her voice shook. She'd heard stories about these men. And seen the naked rage on Sam's face when she'd walked out on him after he tried to force her to kiss him.

Both men stopped as if she had some kind of magic power to keep them from whatever it was they planned.

"Look, Gloria. I need you back on stage. The customers are kicking the door down asking for you. Just come back and sing a few songs. Then we'll be square. You left me in the lurch."

She hid the shoe behind her back and stood to her full height, hoping they didn't notice how much they frightened her. "I told you, Sam. If you tried anything with me, I'd quit."

Vincent took a step closer.

She braced herself.

He put two huge hands around her waist.

She brought the high-heel down on his arm with a sharp crack.

Vincent grunted and tightened his grip.

"Let me go. Get out of here. I called the police and they will be here any minute!" If only she had, the moment she'd seen their auto pull up in front of Rand's cottage. *Oh, God, help me.*

Sam thrust a beefy hand over her mouth. "One way or another you're coming back to the speakeasy. But while we're here—"

"Hold it right there!"

Both men froze.

Gloria tried to wiggle free of the hard hands holding her, but they tightened.

"It's two to one against you, Rand. You don't stand a chance." Vincent tightened his grip on her waist until she found it hard to breathe.

"Don't go for your gun, I know how to use mine." Rand's quiet voice sounded as deadly as his eyes looked. Not a man to be trifled with. A trained combat veteran with experience.

Vincent dropped his hands from her waist.

Sam's arms fell to his side.

She slipped her hand under Sam's suit coat, grasped the handle of his pistol, and pulled the heavy weapon out. As if she knew how to fire the thing, she trained the weapon on the two men. "Now get out!" She hissed.

Vincent probably had a gun, but she feared to get near the man. If he grabbed her and used her for a shield, Rand would be their target. A sick feeling gripped her stomach. She didn't want him hurt.

"Drop your gun, Vincent. Right there on the floor at your feet." Rand's voice held a command the bravest man would have obeyed.

Vincent's glare could have killed her if Rand hadn't been gazing at her with his steady blue eyes.

Vincent inched his gun to the living room floor.

Now what? Rand has just made her enemies his own.

Chapter 11

After the two gangsters left, Rand lowered his weapon and clasped both arms at his sides. He yearned to take the two steps to Gloria and embrace her. Surely, she was as shaken by the encounter as he.

She looked as unflappable as a daredevil before a dangerous stunt. Except her gray eyes looked as somber as a cloudy day.

"I'm so sorry, Rand. I'm afraid you've made some enemies." Her voice trembled.

"You're worried about *me*?" Unbelievable! If he hadn't obeyed his instinct that she needed help, he didn't have to guess what the two gangsters had in mind for her.

"Yes. Sam and Vincent hold grudges. My enemies have become yours." She lowered her hundred-megawatt gaze. "They'll not confront you face to face again. They're better at ambushes and shadows."

"Then my news should be good. A couple barnstormers contacted me and want us to take our show on the road. They've booked at least ten spots for us before winter. How does that strike you?"

"Oh." The clouds in her eyes deepened so her beautiful gaze appeared almost black.

"Not good news?"

"Yes. In a way." She gazed around the cottage living room. "But I've fallen in love with this bungalow. Daisy and I adore living here."

At the mention of her name, Daisy bounded out from behind the couch where she'd evidently hidden when the men with their threatening voices entered. She perched at Rand's feet and gazed up at him with dancing brown eyes.

Rand stooped and rubbed the mutt behind her fluffy ears. "Some watch-dog you are," he teased, giving her a good petting on the head. "Not that I blame you. Those were scary fellas."

"I was hoping to perform a few more shows here, and then see if we could find work somewhere close by." Her mouth trembled.

Blast! Was she about to cry? He took a step toward her. Before he knew what he was about to do, he'd done it. He folded her into his arms, tilted her pert chin up, and planted his lips on her surprisingly responsive ones. Now he'd done it. Crossed the line. Committed himself. He should feel roped in, grounded from all his ambition, tied to the earth. Instead, his head buzzed as if he flew loops and stalls. His heart took flight, warmed and overflowed as if he'd beaten Charlie Lindburgh and broken the world flying record across the Atlantic.

And she melted into his embrace as if she'd been born to snuggle in his arms. He raised his head to gaze down into her captivating, pixie face. The rapturous expression she wore sent lightning bolts flashing through his heart. So this was why men gave up every dream that separated them from the woman they loved? So this was why his father and brothers surrendered their dangerous aspirations. So this was love.

She pulled away. She appeared as wary as a trapeze flyer with a missing net.

How had he been so off-target?

****

Not Rand too! Gloria pulled away. For a moment, she'd let herself be carried away by the safety of his arms and the promise of his lips. Then her brain kicked in. She worked with Rand, and love and employment didn't mix. Not when she needed a steady hand on the wheel to keep a firm foundation under her wing-walking shoes. They had a business agreement. If feelings entered the mix, he'd soon be telling her that she walked too dangerous a tightrope. That she should quit. If he didn't have marriage on his mind, she'd have no option but to leave him and his delightful cottage, and trudge who knew where else searching for a new pilot. And, according to Annie, Rand was definitely *not* the marrying kind.

Nor was she at all certain she wanted to marry him. Though his kiss *had* blown her off-course for an instant until she regained her senses. Marriage needed to be based on far more than strong attraction. Mom and Dad had been so very much in love. Thoughtless about life, but so giddy in love. She would not follow their example and end up as they had. She'd never wish the life she'd lived on an innocent child.

Dear God, why wasn't Rand older and married?

She needed to find a new pilot ASAP. But where?

A knock banged on her door.

She glanced at Rand. He couldn't appear more stunned if he'd been shell-shocked. "Do sit down. We can talk after I see who's at the door."

She waited until Rand sprawled on the chintz couch, and then headed for the door Rand had slammed behind Sam and Vincent when they left.

She opened the door.

A dapper-looking gentlemen stood derby hat in one hand, black leather briefcase in the other, and a smile baring all his white teeth.

"Miss Richards?"

"Yes."

"I'm Jesse Cotton. I'm here representing Adolph Zukor of Paramount Studios in California. May I come in?"

A movie studio? Gloria nodded and pushed open the screen. "Yes, come in."

The man strode in as if he owned the world. "You're a lucky lady. Mr. Zukor saw your wing-walking act several days ago and sent me over with a contract for you to sign. Mr. Zukor wants you to star in his new movie *Wings Over Kitty Hawk.* He admired your act and intends to showcase you with Rudolph Valentino. You've got the looks and the moves he wants in his new movie. He'll pay a grand a week, and the contract is for three months. What do you say, little lady?"

Chapter 12

Rand sucked in a deep breath. He'd just been sucker-punched. Sure, Gloria had the looks to star in movies. And she had the moves on his bi-plane wing. But blast if he wanted her to star in a movie with Valentino. The man seduced every woman who co-starred with him. What women saw in Valentino's sissy looks he couldn't fathom. But to them he seemed irresistible.

And the agent from Paramount had mentioned Douglas Fairbanks as well. What woman could withstand his charm?

He sank into a chintz chair. On the couch opposite him, Jesse Cotton leaned toward Gloria and laid his spiel on thick. Gloria, straight-backed, arms crossed over her chest, her misty gray eyes tracking from Cotton to him and back, listened.

Was she swayed?

Cotton pulled a sheaf of papers from his leather briefcase and handed them over to Gloria. "Sign here and you'll become the biggest female movie star the world has ever embraced."

Gloria leafed through the multiple pages. Turned to the last page and stared at the blanks waiting to be filled in with her signature. "Would I have to move to Hollywood?"

"As soon as possible. Mr. Zukor wants to start filming Monday."

"Isn't this a little fast?" Pink tinted Gloria's cheeks.

"The part was written for Mary Pickford, but she isn't keen to play the action scenes on the wing of a plane." His smile widened to an impossible width. "At first Mr. Zukor envisioned you as a stand-in for the action scenes, but the moment I laid eyes on you, I decided you would star in the film."

"So, Mr. Zukor doesn't know you're signing me as the star rather than the stand-in?"

"Not just yet, little lady. But once he lays eyeballs on you, he'll make you a star."

"But this contract is for the stand-in, not the star."

"We'll negotiate another contract once Mr. Zukor sees you."

"And what of Mary Pickford?"

"Oh, Mr. Zukor has a hand full of other pictures where he can star Mary Pickford." He leaned even closer to Gloria and grabbed her fingers.

She shrank back and pulled her hands away. "Well, certainly I must mull this incredible offer over, Mr. Cotton." She rose, the contract dangling from her hand. "I would like several days to think about this opportunity."

"One day, Miss Richards. Time is of the essence. Certainly twenty-four hours is sufficient time to decide to become a world-famous star. Every girl dreams of being a film star." He put his hand under her chin and tilted her head up. "Especially every girly with the bone structure you have. Our make-up men can jazz you up until the stars can't outshine your luster." He touched her blonde curls. "And this blonde color looks real."

Gloria stepped toward the door. "Thank you, Mr. Cotton." She shifted through the papers in her hand until she located his card. "I'll be in touch."

Unreal. Rand pulled in a deep breath. Any other girl would have signed on the spot. Gloria was no dummy. She would want to go over the contract with a lawyer and then make up her mind. He stood to his feet, his gaze glued to Gloria as she ushered the motion picture agent to her door.

His own offer of touring the country with her walking his wing seemed insignificant now. What girl in her right mind would choose danger to stardom and money? In California she'd be far away from the criminals who threatened her. And she'd no longer have to accept picnics, clam bakes, and fish to ward off hunger.

The door closed behind Mr. Cotton. His

footsteps sounded on the wooden porch, a car door slammed, and an engine sputtered to life.

Gloria turned to him. "What do you think?"

"I'll have my lawyer look over that contract." He held out his hand.

She dropped the papers into his hand. "Thanks. You have a lawyer?"

"Yeah." He swallowed. She was his angel. Walked his wing. He didn't want to lose her. He gripped the contract. In that stark moment, her face with her incredible eyes etched into his brain. He couldn't lose her.

Warmth arched between them like sparks from a bonfire.

Yet he wouldn't clip her wings if she wanted to fly to the stars.

And he was more certain than Jesse Cotton of Paramount Studios that she could.

Chapter 13

A door banged.

Gloria parted the kitchen curtain and gazed toward Rand's cottage. His long-legged gait took him quickly through the picket gate, up the path, and onto her porch. Finally!

She checked her lipstick once more and fluffed her hair. Gathering dusk darkened her living room so she flicked on the new electric lights. Daisy thwacked her tail on the polished wooden floor, not barking as she did for strangers because she knew Rand's step.

Gloria smoothed her white dress to her knees. She felt like a finch fluffing its feathers. She'd been on pins and needles all day. What would his lawyer say about the contract? What would Rand say about her moving to California and starring with Rudolph Valentino?

She ran to answer his familiar knock. Her heart beat as fast as a propeller on take-off.

He stepped inside and handed her the contract.

"Well, what did your lawyer say?"

"It's on the up and up. Well-drawn and covers every aspect of your being the stand-in for Mary Pickford."

She motioned to the couch. "Come, sit next to me. Tell me everything."

"Not much to tell. Cotton told you what he thought about your being a star, and if you want that, I think he'll draw up a new contract making you the star of *Wings Over Kitty Hawk*."

Rand's smile appeared carved from granite. His lapis blue eyes had darkened to almost black. Even when he'd been blasted with his worst headaches, he'd never looked so grim.

Her heart hurt for him.

"The question is, is that what *you* want?" His back rigid, his arms stiff at his side, he perched on the edge of the couch, his knee touching hers.

She could be a star if she wanted. Did she? She'd thought all day of what she'd gain. Money, fame, freedom. She'd tasted fame and the glory satisfied. For a moment. But the euphoric feeling faded. She'd been free all her life. But freedom didn't buy friends. Or family. Did fame mean she'd not feel insignificant anymore? Did fame bring love? She'd lost everyone she'd ever loved. Money had never been important, except when she'd had none for food.

“I’m not sure.” She glanced around the cozy bungalow. “I’ve been so content here.” Did being a movie star bring happiness? According to the snippets of news she’d read about the stars, being on the screen didn’t guarantee happiness.

“If you want to be a famous movie star, I’ll call Cotton and arrange for a new contract.”

Rand’s voice sounded so hollow. Why?

“Actually, I think I’d like to live right here and be your wing-walker.”

“But the gangsters?”

Was that a sparkle returning to those blue, blue eyes of his? “You’ll be here to protect me, won’t you?”

Rand’s expression lit like the fireworks she’d once seen at the fairgrounds.

“You want to stay here? At Kitty Hawk?” His strong fingers twined around hers, sending sparks of warmth though her body.

“Yes. I’m happy here. Just Daisy and me.”

Was she telling the truth? Why hadn’t she realized that she carried a torch for Rand? He’d been here for her whenever she needed him. And from day one, her heart beat faster and her stomach fluttered every time he was near. She counted on him every time they took to the skies. Her life was in his hands. She *trusted* him. Well, if she was really truthful, she *liked* him. Actually, now that stardom had lost all its luster for her, she could admit to herself that maybe, just maybe, she loved Rand.

He must have read something in her expression, because his entire posture changed. In front of her eyes, he relaxed.

He slid down to the floor and knelt at her side. He slipped his hand inside his coat pocket and pulled out a rather large, cardboard sign. And held it up for her to read.

Maitland and Maitland, the lowest-flying, most daredevil aviation acrobats in the world.

"What's this?" Her heart beat faster.

He slid his other hand into his coat pocket and brought out a ring box. He lifted the lid and held his offering out to her.

She gasped. "Oh, my. That's beautiful. Can you afford that?"

"Gloria Richards, will you do me the honor of becoming my wife?"

Yes, she loved him. "But your dream? You want to make that first solo flight across the Atlantic."

"Dreams are dreams. What I feel for you is real. I love you, Gloria." His eyes widened as if he'd just discovered some new truth. "I guess I loved you from the moment I first saw you with your ridiculous red high heels flailing in the sand."

"And I love you too! Yes, I'll be overjoyed to marry you."

"And—"

"But I don't want you to surrender your dream. I'll support you all the way as you fly across the Atlantic and beat Charlie Lindburgh."

"We'll see about that." He flashed his to-die-for

smile. "But you're giving up your chance at fame and fortune. And there's no danger in performing for the big screen."

She didn't need more fame. Danger had always been part of her life. Now she flew into a safe harbor. This was the meaning of life. What she'd been searching for her entire life. To love and to be loved. She wanted nothing more.

"You may decide not to be a star of the silver screen, but you'll always star in my life."

His kiss sent her soaring into the clouds.

"Being a movie star has never been my dream. Since I lost my parents I've searched for love and a home and family of my own, with a little excitement thrown in." She tilted back her head and laughed, tears threatening to gather in her eyes. She blinked them back. "Now I've found my dream." Her voice broke. "*You* are my dream. No way I'm leaving you for Hollywood!"

Thank You, Father God, now I have a place to call home. Thank You for love! I have the love of one good man. I don't need the adulation of crowds.

Dear Reader,

I so hope you enjoyed DAREDEVILS, included in this FIFTY STATES-NORTH CAROLINA Anthology, as much as I loved writing the novella. And I'm certain you will love the other stories as well.

I've written several other novellas. You might want to read my novellas *Keara's Escape* included in the ORPHAN TRAIN series, *Recipe For A Husband*, included in the THANKSGIVING Anthology, and *A Fool For Love* included in the APRIL FOOL LOVE Anthology. I think you will also love my novella titled *A Groom For Christmas,* included in the MULLED CHRISTMAS KISSES Anthology, and my novella, *A Christmas Belle,* included in the CHRISTMAS MAIL ORDER ANGELS Anthology. My novella, *The Marriage Broker and The Mortician*, published by Barbour is included in THE CALIFORNIA GOLD RUSH ROMANCE COLLECTION. If you enjoy novellas, I'm certain you will like these other books.

I find it such a pleasure to speak with my readers. I hope you will visit with me at www.AnneGreeneAuthor.com, www.facebook.com/AnneWGreeneAuthor, on twitter @TheAnneGreene, and on Pinterest at The Anne Greene. I enjoy discovering what you think about my books and about other Christian books you love.

I'm expecting to hear from you, and hope I won't be disappointed. If you'd like to subscribe to my newsletter, please drop me an email at annewgreene@gmail.com.

Thank you for reading Daredevils. Please consider telling your friends or posting a short review on Amazon or Good Reads. Word of mouth is an author's best friend and much appreciated.

Books by Anne Greene

Angel with Steel Wings

Holly Garden, PI: Red Is for Rookie

Masquerade Marriage

Marriage By Arrangement

A Texas Christmas Mystery

A Christmas Belle (Christmas Mail Order Angels)

April Fool's Love

Christmas Mail Order Angels: The complete 11 Volume Set

The California Gold Rush Romance Collection: 9 Stories of Finding Treasures Worth More than Gold

Warm Mulled Kisses: A Collection of 10 Christian Christmas Novellas

Anne Greene Author Home Page

ABOUT THE AUTHOR

ANNE GREENE BIO

My home is in the quaint antiquing town of McKinney, Texas, just a few miles north of Dallas. My dear husband is a retired Colonel, Army Special Forces. We recently returned from a two-year stint at Yongson Garrison in Seoul, Korea. My little brown and white Shih Tzu, Lily Valentine, shares my writing space, curled at my feet. I have four beautiful, talented children, and eight grandchildren who keep me running.

I've travelled to every location of each book I've written and each book is a book of my heart. Besides my first love, writing, I enjoy travel, art, sports, reading, sailing, snorkeling, movies, and way too many other things to mention. Life is good. Jesus said, "I am come that you might have life and that you might have it more abundantly." Whether writing contemporary or historical, my books celebrate the abundant life Jesus gives.

Moody Press published my first book, ***Trail of Tears***. I love writing about alpha heroes who aren't afraid to fall on their knees in prayer, and about gutsy heroines. My ***Women of Courage series*** spotlights heroic women of World War II. You might want to begin with the first book ***Angel With Steel Wings.*** Read my private investigating series, ***Handcuffed In Texas.*** The first book is ***Red Is For Rookie.*** Enjoy my award-winning Scottish historical romances, ***Masquerade Marriage*** and ***Marriage By Arrangement.*** I trust my stories transport you to awesome new worlds and touch your heart to seek a deeper spiritual relationship with the Lord Jesus. Buy my books on http://www.Amazon.com.

77084494R10063

Made in the USA
Columbia, SC
22 September 2017